The Mystery
of the
Manor Jewels

About the Author

Dominick Tobin was born and educated in County Dublin. He works in the Civil Service and is married and has four children. Dominick and his family lived for eight years in Mullingar, before returning to Dublin where he now lives. *The Mystery of the Manor Jewels* is his first book for children.

The Mystery
of the
Manor Jewels

DOMINICK TOBIN

POOLBEG

For my children –
Ciaran, Niall, Mairead and Sinead
– thanks for the inspiration

Published in 1995 by
Poolbeg Press Ltd,
Knocksedan House,
123 Baldoyle Industrial Estate,
Dublin 13, Ireland

© Dominick Tobin 1995

The moral right of the author has been asserted.

A catalogue record for this book is available from the British Library.

ISBN 1 85371 445 3

Cover illustration by Michael Mascaro
Cover design by Poolbeg Group Services Ltd
Set by Poolbeg Group Services Ltd in Palatino 12/15
Printed by The Guernsey Press Ltd,
Vale, Guernsey, Channel Islands.

Contents

1

The Secret Compartment

"Why do we have to live here?" complained Steve.

His mother sighed.

"I've already explained that to you," she said.

"Well I hate it here," grumbled Steve.

"You knew we would have to move when your father got his new job," his mother explained.

"What was wrong with his old job?" asked Steve.

"This is a better job," his mother told him.

"I liked our old house. I had friends there," said Steve.

"You'll have friends here, just give it a chance."

"I have given it a chance and I don't like it," insisted Steve.

"Look, there's no use arguing about it. We're here now and we're here to stay. Just make the best of it," his mother said firmly.

Steve didn't answer.

"Why don't you go up to your room and put your things away," suggested his mother.

Steve trudged slowly up the stairs. He hated this house. He hated his room.

He kicked open the bedroom door. In the middle of the floor boxes of books, toys and clothes waited to be unpacked. Across the room stood the large wooden wardrobe which took up one wall of his room. He hated that wardrobe.

Steve picked up the box containing his electric train set. It had been set up in his old house, but now it was packed away in a box.

"I'll put it on the shelf in the corner of the wardrobe until I have time to set it up again," he decided.

He flung open the door, and standing on tiptoes hoisted the box up over his head and pushed it along the shelf.

The box slid in halfway and then stopped. Steve pushed harder, but the box wouldn't move. He took the box down and looked at it.

It should fit, he thought.

He slid the box along the shelf again. Again it stuck.

"There must be something behind it," said Steve to himself.

He took the box down again and, climbing on a chair, he felt along the shelf. His hand soon hit the back of the wardrobe.

Steve was puzzled.

The bottom part of the wardrobe was deep enough to walk into. So why was the shelf so narrow? He peered along the shelf, but it was dark in the wardrobe and he couldn't see anything.

Again he put his hand in and felt around. This time his hand came to rest on something small and round. It was a knob.

Steve pulled the knob firmly and the back of the shelf swung open like a door.

He slid his hand into the small compartment behind the door. His fingers came to rest against something hard and cold. Slowly he pulled the object towards him. When it reached the edge of the shelf he could see it was a green coloured tin, about half the size of a biscuit tin. The lid of the tin was covered in thick cobwebs.

As Steve lifted the tin down to the floor for closer examination, a spider jumped for freedom, ran across the floor and escaped to safety under the wardrobe.

With the tips of his fingers, Steve brushed away the cobwebs. There had been writing on the lid, but it was now too faded to read.

Carefully he began to lift the lid. It creaked in protest, and for a second Steve felt like a grave robber. He pulled harder. Suddenly the lid came free with a groan.

There was a book with a blue cover packed neatly inside. Steve lifted it out carefully.

The writing on the cover of the book was faded, but he could still just make it out. The name "James Clarke" was written across the top, and below it the address: Riverside Cottage,

Cedar Avenue, Monksfield.

"He lived here," said Steve, "he must have forgotten to bring this with him when they moved."

Steve began to lift the cover, then he closed it again.

Maybe I shouldn't read it, he thought.

For a few seconds he did nothing, then he lifted the cover again.

"He should have brought it with him," he decided.

The writing on the page wasn't faded like the cover and Steve found it easy to read.

"20th March" was written across the top of the first page. "Today is my 13th birthday . . ."

"That makes him three months older than me," Steve calculated.

> Aunt Sarah gave me this diary for my birthday.
> I will keep it in a safe place . . . Tom forgot his
> school books today. Mr Nolan was very angry . . .

The diary went on and on, mostly about school. Steve began to get bored. He was just about to close the diary when the writing at the top right-hand corner of the page caught his eye.

"How did I miss that?" wondered Steve in amazement.

It was the date. Steve had only read "20th March". He hadn't looked across the page, and now he could hardly believe his eyes. There, written in big black figures was the year: 1914!

2

The Diary

Steve nearly dropped the diary with surprise.

"1914! James Clarke was thirteen years old in 1914!" he exclaimed. "That makes him older than Grandad."

The diary suddenly became more interesting.

Steve skipped through the pages. He read an entry here and there. The months passed by. Summer came, and with it the school holidays.

10th June: I had nothing to do today, so I went down to the rail depot to have a look around. The depot is a very busy place these days. The Railway are building a new platform and there are a lot of men working on it.

While I was there it started to rain, so I went into a shed near the waiting-room for shelter. The workmen must use the shed as a tea room, because there were cups and bread and even a packet of biscuits on the table.

I was just about to take a biscuit when I heard some men approaching. I looked around for somewhere to hide and saw a ladder in the corner of the shed. I climbed up the ladder. It led to a loft full of boxes and buckets and old tools and I found a good hiding-place behind one of the boxes. Nobody could see me there, but I could see and hear everything.

The workmen came into the shed for a cup of tea and sat around talking. I know most of them to see. They are all locals . . .

The front door opened, as Steve's father came in from work.

"Steve, it's time for dinner," his mother shouted up the stairs.

I'll read more of this later, Steve decided. He closed the diary and put it under his pillow for safe-keeping.

By the time Steve got down to the kitchen, his father was already sitting at the table eating his dinner.

"How did you get on in your new job?" Steve asked him.

"Fine, just fine," his father replied. "It was the best move I ever made."

Maybe it was for you and Mum, thought Steve, but it certainly wasn't for me.

He glanced into his father's plate and screwed up his face at the sight of meat, vegetables and potatoes.

"What's for dinner?" he asked hesitantly.

"Don't worry," his mother reassured him, "I have a burger and chips for you."

Steve sighed with relief. No matter what he did with meat and vegetables they never tasted as good as a burger and chips.

"Did you make any friends yet?" asked his father.

"How can he make friends when he never leaves the house?" his mother pointed out. "He spends the day watching television."

"I went out today," said Steve defensively.

"Only for fifteen minutes," added his mother

"I thought it was going to rain," said Steve, and I just remembered that there was a programme I wanted to see on the telly, he thought to himself.

"Maybe he'll make friends and go out more when he starts school," suggested his father.

"Talking about school, have you everything ready for tomorrow?" his mother asked.

"Yes, Mum," replied Steve. He had almost forgotten that he was starting in his new school in the morning. He hated the thought of it.

He finished his dinner, dropped his fork on to the empty plate and stood up from the table.

"I think I'll go to bed early," he said, as he headed back upstairs to his bedroom.

Steve took the diary from under his pillow and hopped into bed. He flicked through the pages and started to read again.

16th June: The heavy rain continues. Dad says it is the wettest June he can remember.

The river is at its highest level ever and if the rain doesn't stop soon there is a danger that it will burst its banks.

21st June: The rain stopped at last and just in time for the Earl of Monksfield's midsummer picnic on the Manor lawn. There was a Punch and Judy show and free sweets and lemonade for the children.

As usual, my dad refused to go. He says the Earl should pay his workers a decent wage and come down to the town and see how people have to live, instead of sitting on the hill in his big house.

3rd July: There was a big meeting in the church hall this evening. A man from Redmond's Nationalist Party came to talk about Home Rule. But a group of Republicans at the back of the hall kept heckling him and the meeting ended in uproar. My dad says that it is going to split the country . . .

Steve skipped a few more pages.

13th July: I was in the shed in the rail depot today. All the talk is of the war. John Conroy says he is going to join up. His younger brother David is in my class . . .

Steve yawned. He was beginning to feel bored again, but the next entry in the diary soon revived his interest.

15th July: I was in the loft of the shed again this afternoon. It was very quiet. Nothing was happening.

I was just about to go home when four men came in. I know them all to see; Jim Barry, Noel Rogers, Sam King and Jack Stone. Stone is a bad man. He has often been in trouble with the police.

Stone closed the shed door and then the four of them gathered round and began to talk in low voices. They never saw me and I heard every word they said.

'What do we do now?' asked King.

'We can't walk around wearing jewels,' said Rogers.

'That's for sure,' agreed Barry.

'So what do we do?' asked King again.

Up to this point Stone hadn't spoken. The three other men now looked to him for leadership.

'We'll leave the jewels where they are,' Stone told them.

'Will they be safe?' asked a worried-looking King.

'Without the map I wouldn't be able to find them myself,' Stone reassured him.

'That's right,' Barry nodded in agreement.

'Will we be able to find the map again?' asked Rogers.

'Of course we will,' said Stone. 'It's the only oak tree on the Manor estate.'

'What if somebody else finds it?' asked King. 'I mean isn't it dangerous to hide the map so close to the Manor?'

'That's why nobody will find it,' said Stone confidently. 'Nobody will think of looking there. Anyway the hole is five feet high. You have to put your hand in and up to the left. It's perfectly safe.'

'When do we go back for the jewels?' asked Rogers.

'On this day in two years' time. We'll all meet here at midnight,' Stone told them. 'Now let's get out of here before somebody comes.'

Barry, King and Rogers left the shed. Stone was the last to leave. I watched as he closed the door behind him.

Suddenly a mouse darted out from the corner of the loft and ran across my hand. I jumped in fright, and knocked over a rusty lamp.

Stone must have heard the noise because he came back into the shed.

I pushed myself closer to the floor. I didn't dare to look. I could hear his footsteps as he walked across the shed floor and stopped directly below me. I held my breath and prayed silently.

Stone moved towards the ladder that led to the loft.

I began to panic.

What'll I do? Will I jump? Will I run? What'll I do? The questions ran through my mind, but still I lay on the loft floor, frozen with fear.

Stone began to climb the steps. One . . . two . . . three . . . I pushed myself closer to the floor. My heart began to pound.

'What's wrong?' asked a voice from the shed door. It was King. He had come back to see what had happened to Stone.

'I heard a noise,' said Stone.

'What was it?' asked King.

'I don't know,' said Stone, 'but it came from the loft.'

Stone climbed another step and then another. Two more steps and he would be in the loft.

'It was probably just a bird,' suggested King.

Stone stopped climbing, but didn't answer.

'Come on,' urged King, 'we'd better go. The workmen will be back soon.'

There was a long pause, it seemed to go on forever, before Stone finally made up his mind.

'OK,' he agreed reluctantly, 'you're probably right.'

Stone climbed back down the ladder and walked across the shed to the door. He stopped and had another long look around before he left the shed and closed the door behind him.

I let out my breath in a slow sigh of relief.

For a few moments I lay still on the floor, until at last my pounding heart returned to normal.

I climbed down the ladder as fast as I could and peered out the shed door. There was nobody around. Quickly I slipped out of the shed, ran through the depot and back to the road.

As I walked home, I saw Stone standing at a street corner. I crossed the road to avoid him. I could feel him staring at me. He made me feel uncomfortable, but I'm sure he didn't see me in the loft.

Dad was full of chat tonight at supper. He says the robbery is the talk of the town. The police have no idea who did it.

I was about to tell him what I had overheard, but decided to wait.

Tomorrow I shall go to the Manor estate and look for the map.

Steve turned the page. He was eager to know if James Clarke had found the map, but the page was blank. He turned the next page. It was also blank. So was the next page and the next. He flicked through the rest of the diary. All the pages were empty

"There are no more entries," said Steve to himself. "I wonder what happened?"

3

A New Friend

"It's time to get up, Steve. Time to get up. You'll be late for school."

His mother's voice echoed round and round in Steve's head. Slowly he opened one eye and then the other. He reached out a hand and picked up his watch from the side of the bed. One glance at it confirmed what his mother had told him. It was time to get up. Steve gave one last yawn, flung back the covers and jumped out of bed.

A blue book landed on the floor with a thud. It was the diary. Suddenly the memory of everything he had read the night before flooded back into Steve's mind.

Did James Clarke go to Monksfield Manor to search for the map? Did he go looking for the jewels? Why did he suddenly stop writing in his diary?

There were a lot of questions that needed answers and Steve was determined to find those answers.

I'll have to find out what happened, he decided.

A few minutes later, Steve appeared in the kitchen washed and dressed.

"Where's Dad?" he asked.

"Gone to work," replied his mother, "and you should be gone to school."

Steve glanced at his watch. He couldn't understand why his mother was so excited. This was the way he always got ready for school. Anyway, he was in no hurry this morning. He hated the thought of starting a new school.

Maybe I should pretend I'm sick, he thought.

He glanced up at his mother, but the look on her face told Steve that she wouldn't believe him.

After a bowl of cornflakes and two slices of toast and marmalade, he was ready for school.

"Is my lunch made?" he asked.

"It's in your bag," his mother told him.

"I suppose I'd better go," said Steve.

He waited for his mother to say that he could stay home, but she didn't.

"Are you sure you don't want me to come with you?" she asked instead.

"I'm sure," Steve replied. It was bad enough starting in a new school. If his mother came along it would only make things worse.

It was a lonely walk to the school and even lonelier in the school yard. Groups of boys huddled together, playing and talking. Steve had nobody to talk to. He wished he was back in his old school. He wished he was in his old yard with the friends he knew.

When the bell rang the boys lined up in their usual lines and waited to be called to their classes.

Steve had been told to report to the Headmaster's office. He had been there before, when his mother had brought him to register. Slowly he trudged across the yard to the Reception area. He turned the handle on the large brown door and stepped into a long corridor. It felt cold and he shivered.

A sign on the door opposite him read "Headmaster's Office". Steve wondered whether he should knock. What he really wanted to do was run away, away from the school, away from the town.

Just as he lifted his hand to rap on the door, it swung open and the Headmaster's short, square and bald shape appeared in the doorway.

When Steve had come to register with his mother, the headmaster had been smiling; now he was scowling.

"What is it, son?" he asked impatiently.

"Daly, Sir. Steve Daly," Steve replied politely.

Steve waited for a response, but the Headmaster just looked at him blankly. Steve could see that his name meant nothing to him. "I'm starting here today, Sir," added Steve.

"Oh, of course. The new boy." At last the Headmaster remembered. "Just wait here and

I'll be back to you in a minute," he said.

Steve leaned against the corridor wall. The Headmaster waddled down the corridor on his stumpy legs before disappearing around the corner.

A minute went by, then another and another. Fifteen minutes had passed and still the Headmaster hadn't returned.

He must have forgotten about me, thought Steve, but just then the Headmaster reappeared with a bundle of papers under his arm.

"You'll be in Mr Grant's class," he puffed breathlessly. "That's room fourteen. Follow me."

The Headmaster led the way until they came to a faded brown door with the number 14 written on it.

From inside the room came the sound of voices. A deeper voice shouted at them to be quiet.

The Headmaster knocked at the door, then entered without waiting for a reply.

Immediately the class went quiet. The boys opened their books and began to read. Even the grey-haired man who had been trying to teach them looked uncomfortable.

"This is Steve Daly," said the Headmaster. "He has come down from the city to live in our little town. I am putting him in your class, Mr Grant.

"Very good, Headmaster." The teacher nodded his grey head in agreement.

The Headmaster left the room as quickly as he had entered. The boys relaxed again and a smile appeared on the teacher's face.

"Now, where will I put you?" Mr Grant asked himself the question.

Steve glanced around the room. Suspicious and unfriendly eyes stared back at him. At the back of the class, a thin-faced boy with round glasses gave him a welcoming smile.

"Ah! There's a free desk in front of Maurice Brady," declared Mr Grant. He pointed to an empty desk in the second row, in front of an unfriendly-looking red-haired boy.

Steve had just sat down when something sharp stuck into his back.

"So you think you're a tough guy from the city?" growled Brady. "Just wait until lunchtime."

Steve didn't bother replying. There was no point in talking to boys like Brady. He thought about telling Mr Grant, but that would only make matters worse.

At one o'clock the bell rang for lunch and the boys streamed out of the classroom.

Steve spotted an empty bench in the corner of the yard and decided to have his lunch there.

He had just taken the jam sandwich from his lunch box when Maurice Brady arrived. He was followed by a group of boys.

This must be his gang, thought Steve.

"You're sitting on my bench," snarled Brady.

There was plenty of room on the next bench,

so Steve got up to move.

"You're not very brave, are you?" jeered Brady. He pushed Steve and the gang laughed.

A large group of boys had now gathered around to see what was happening.

"I don't want to fight," said Steve. He tried to walk past Brady, but Brady stood in his way.

"Well *I* want to fight," said Brady, and he pushed Steve again.

This time he pushed harder than the first. Steve staggered back. His sandwich fell from his hand and landed in the dirt.

Brady and his gang laughed again. Steve looked down at his sandwich. He was hungry, and he had been looking forward to eating it. Now he would have no lunch.

Steve looked up at Brady's leering face, then something strange happened.

His left arm seemed to have a mind of its own. Suddenly, it shot up from his side and crashed into the side of Brady's face. Brady was sent sprawling to the ground.

The gang looked on in disbelief, while Brady sat on the ground sobbing and rubbing his jaw.

"Well done, Steve," came a voice from behind.

Steve turned around. It was the thin-faced boy with the round glasses.

"You won't have any more trouble from him," said the boy. "By the way, my name's Simon Hughes."

"Won't he tell the Head?" asked Steve.

"Not likely," said Simon. "Anyway, I saw the whole thing. Brady started it."

A small dark-haired boy carrying a lunch box came up to Steve. "My Mum always packs too many sandwiches," he said. "You can have one if you like."

"Thanks," said Steve.

That afternoon Steve was treated like an old friend by the rest of the class. They all smiled and made him feel welcome. All except Maurice Brady. He was still rubbing his sore jaw.

Finally the bell rang and it was time to go home.

"Where do you live?" asked Simon.

"Riverside Cottage, on Cedar Avenue," Steve told him.

"I go home that way," said Simon. "I'll go with you to the end of my road."

The boys had a long chat as they walked home. Steve was surprised at how much they had in common.

At the end of Simon's road they parted company. "See you in the morning," called Simon, as they waved good-bye.

Steve whistled to himself as he walked down his road. Somehow he was beginning to feel very much at home in Monksfield.

It might not be too bad here after all, he thought.

4

Footsteps in the Night

Steve was up early the following morning.

His mother was surprised to see him arrive down for breakfast before she had even called him.

"Why are you up so early?" she asked.

"I couldn't sleep," Steve answered truthfully.

"Are you worried about school?" his mother asked.

"No," said Steve.

He had been thinking about James Clarke's diary again. He had to find out what had happened to him, but he didn't know where to start. The only person he knew well enough to trust was Simon. So he had decided to ask him.

It was lunch-time before Steve got a chance to talk to Simon. The two boys were sitting on a bench having their lunch together when Steve brought up the subject.

"Where would I find out about local history?" he asked.

Simon laughed. "There's not much history around here," he said. "Nothing ever happens in Monksfield."

"I want to find out about the people who lived in our house before us," said Steve.

"There hasn't been anybody living there for ages," Simon told him, "but my dad would know who the last people were."

"I want to know about a person who lived there a long time ago," said Steve.

"Why?" asked Simon.

Steve glanced around the yard to make sure that nobody else could hear him.

"Will you promise you won't tell anybody?" he whispered.

"Promise," whispered Simon in return.

"I found a diary," said Steve.

"What kind of diary?" asked Simon.

"It was written by a boy who lived in the house," Steve told him.

"When?" asked Simon.

Steve glanced around the yard again. There was nobody near enough to hear.

"In 1914," he told Simon.

"Wow!" exclaimed Simon. "What's in it?"

"I'll tell you later," said Steve, "but I want to know what happened to the boy who wrote it."

"Mrs Faulkner, the local librarian, would be the best person to ask," decided Simon. "She knows everything about local history. She even wrote a book about it. We can go and see her after school."

"OK," agreed Steve.

That afternoon the boys went to the library.

On the way, Steve told Simon what was written in the diary.

Simon could hardly believe his ears.

"So James Clarke overheard the robbers talking and knew where the map was hidden," exclaimed Simon.

"That's right," said Steve

"What happened to him?" wondered Simon. "Did he ever find the map?"

"That's what we are going to try to find out," said Steve.

"Even if James Clarke didn't find the map, it couldn't still be there," said Simon.

"Why not?" asked Steve.

"Monksfield Manor is just a ruin now. There are houses built on the estate. The tree was probably cleared away years ago," Simon told him.

Steve was disappointed, but he still wanted to find out what had happened to James Clarke.

Mrs Faulkner was putting away books when the boys arrived at the library.

"Good afternoon, boys," she greeted them warmly.

"This is Steve Daly," said Simon. "He's new to Monksfield and would like to know about local history."

Steve could see from Mrs Faulkner's face that she was thrilled with the request.

"Local history is my favourite subject," she said.

"Steve is living in Riverside Cottage, on Cedar Avenue," explained Simon.

"I'm interested in the history of the house and the people who lived in it," said Steve. "Simon said you could help."

"How far do you want to go back?" asked Mrs Faulkner.

"To the beginning of the century, if possible," said Steve.

Mrs Faulkner thought for a moment.

"I might be able to help," she said. "Wait there."

Mrs Faulkner disappeared through a door at the back of the library. She returned a few minutes later carrying a pile of large dusty books.

"We'll sit here," she said, and put the books down on a table beside the main desk.

"Mr Vaughan, the County Registrar, has kindly let me have these books for my research," explained Mrs Faulkner. She spread the books out in front of the boys.

"Now let me see," she said, as she looked at the books. "Ah, here we are, Monksfield Parish records, 1892 to 1908."

The boys looked on eagerly as Mrs Faulkner began to turn the pages. She stopped at a page headed Cedar Avenue. Her finger ran down the page until she came to Riverside Cottage.

"Here we are," she said. "In 1892 the house was occupied by James and Martha Clarke. The following year it's the same, and the year after, the next year . . ." Mrs Faulkners's voice trailed off.

"Ah! Here's a change," she said. "20th March 1901, a boy, also called James, was born."

"Could I start my research by checking what happened to him?" asked Steve hopefully.

"Certainly," said Mrs Faulkner. "I'll check the *Births, Marriages and Deaths* Register."

She opened another large book and began to flick through the pages until she came to "Clarke".

"Here he is," she said. "James Clarke, born Monksfield 20th March 1901, died Newcastle 8th April 1973."

"Did he have a family?" asked Steve.

"No. He wasn't married," said Mrs Faulkner.

Steve was disappointed. Now I'll never know what happened to him, he thought.

"There is something very familiar about his name," said Mrs Faulkner after a while, "but I can't think what it is."

She got up from the table and went behind the desk. She returned with a book entitled *The History of Monksfield*.

"I wrote this book myself," she explained. "I'll see if his name is in the index."

Steve crossed his fingers and waited in hope, while Mrs Faulkner checked the index.

"He's here," she confirmed, "page 96."

She sat down at the table again and opened

the book to page 96.

"Now I remember," she said. "I did some research on him."

The boys glanced at each other and waited for Mrs Faulkner to continue.

"It was a strange incident," she said finally.

"What happened?" asked Steve eagerly.

Mrs Faulkner sat back in her chair, as if preparing to tell a long story.

"It was just before war broke out," she began, "the First World War, that is. There was a big robbery at Monksfield Manor. At that time the Manor was a large country estate. Jewels valued at £2000 were stolen."

"How much would they be worth now?" asked Simon.

Mrs Faulkner thought for a moment.

"I suppose they would be worth over £100,000 now," she said.

"£100,000!" echoed Simon in amazement.

"Were the jewels ever recovered?" asked Steve.

"No," said Mrs Faulkner, "and the thieves were never caught.

"Anyway," she continued, "the day following the robbery, this boy, James Clarke, disappeared. A huge search was organised. Everybody in the town helped. The river was dragged and the quarry searched. Boats even searched the harbour, but there was no trace of the boy. Everybody thought he was dead, but a week later he turned up in Brookfield, which is twelve miles away. He had a large bump on his head, but no other injuries. Nobody ever found out how he had got there. He had completely lost his memory and never recovered it again. He didn't even know his own name or recognise his parents."

Mrs Faulkner closed the books and got up from the table.

"I must get back to work now," she said. "Just ask if you need to know anything else. There were a lot of articles about James Clarke and the robbery in the newspapers at the time. They're all stored here. I'll get them out for you if you want to call back in a few days."

"Thanks very much for your help," said the boys.

"At least now we know what happened to James Clarke," said Simon on the way home.

"We still don't know what happened to the map," said Steve.

They stopped for a moment at the end of Simon's road.

"After school tomorrow I'm going out to the Manor to look for the oak tree," decided Steve.

"You'll be wasting your time," said Simon.

"I'm going anyway," insisted Steve.

"In that case, I'm going with you," said Simon.

"OK," agreed Steve, "I'll see you in school tomorrow."

That night Steve tossed and turned in bed. He kept thinking about James Clarke and wondering what had happened to him.

He had only just closed his eyes when the room began to spin. Round and round it spun, faster and faster. Steve felt himself being lifted from his bed. He seemed to be floating somewhere near the ceiling, looking down at his own bedroom.

The door opened and a boy walked in. He went over to the wardrobe, took out the diary and carried it over to a desk in the corner of the room.

A desk – where did that come from? wondered Steve.

The boy wrote something in the diary, but Steve couldn't see what he had written. He put the diary back in the wardrobe, then left the bedroom and walked down the stairs.

Steve could feel himself being sucked down the stairs after the boy. Suddenly he was no longer looking down on the boy, he *was* the boy.

He reached the bottom of the stairs and opened the front door. Outside it wasn't quite dark, but it wasn't bright either. It was a sort of strange half-light.

Steve started to walk down the road, but he didn't seem to be going anywhere in particular.

A shuffling noise behind him made him spin round, but he couldn't see anything. He walked on a little further. Again he heard the noise. This time he recognised it. It was the sound of footsteps. Again, he spun round, but he couldn't see anything.

Steve began to walk a little faster. The footsteps followed and seemed to be getting closer.

Faster and faster he walked. His breathing became shallow and quick, his heart pounded in his chest as he pushed himself faster and faster. Still the footsteps followed. They seemed to be below him, beside him, across the road from him and getting closer and closer . . .

Steve sat up in bed gasping. He took a long deep breath to steady his thumping heart.

What a strange dream, he thought.

Just as he lay down again he heard a sound which sent a shiver through him. It was the sound of footsteps.

I must be imagining it, he thought. But no, there it was again. It wasn't his imagination. It was the sound of footsteps right outside his bedroom window.

Steve glanced at his watch. It was three am.

He jumped out of bed and went over to the window. Across the street, a man moved carefully in the shadows of the buildings. Suddenly a car sped around the corner. The man tried to hide his face, but he was too slow. He was caught in the full glare of the car's lights.

Steve recognised him immediately. It was Mr Walker, who had just moved in to Mrs Gray's guest-house down the road.

"Where is he going at this time of night?" wondered Steve.

5

The Search for the Oak Tree

The next morning, Steve had forgotten all about Walker. His thoughts were taken up with the search for the oak tree on the Manor estate.

"Are you still coming along this afternoon?" Steve asked Simon at lunchtime.

"Of course," replied Simon. "I wouldn't miss it for anything."

After school, the boys waited for the number 17 bus, which would take them to Monksfield Manor.

"There won't be much chance of finding the oak tree," said Simon doubtfully.

"If we don't look we'll never find the jewels, or find out what happened to James Clarke," said Steve. He was determined to do everything possible to solve the mystery.

When the bus arrived it was packed and the boys had to stand. Luckily the journey wasn't long. After ten minutes the bus groaned to a halt beside two large stone pillars.

"We're here," said Simon.

The boys squeezed their way off the bus and

out into the fresh air.

"Where do we start?" asked Simon.

"What we need is to find a hill or piece of high ground so that we can overlook the estate," decided Steve.

Simon thought for a minute.

"I know just the place," he said. "I played a football match with the school here last year. You can see the whole estate from the pitch."

"That sounds just right," said Steve.

Simon led the way down Manor Avenue until they came to a road called Manor Rise. At the side of the road there was a sign which read "Pitch."An arrow on the sign pointed up the road.

"It's just up here," he said.

"They named this road correctly," panted Steve, as they trudged up the steep hill.

At last they reached the football pitch.

"Over there," said Steve, when he got his breath back. He pointed to a small hill behind one of the goals. "That's the highest point."

From the top of the hill the boys were able to look down over the whole estate. In the centre of the estate was Monksfield Manor, now in ruins. All around it rows and rows of houses had been built.

The boys could see the gardens, the roads and the open green spaces, but there was no sign of a big oak tree.

Simon sighed with disappointment.

"Well that's it," he said. "The oak tree is gone."

Steve also felt disappointed, but he wasn't going to give up the search just yet.

"We'll take a quick look through the estate," he said.

"For what?" asked Simon. "If we can't see the oak tree from here we'll never find it among all those houses."

"Just a quick look," persisted Steve, "until the bus comes."

"OK," agreed Simon reluctantly.

The boys went back down Manor Rise, up to the top of Manor Avenue, across Manor Park and down Manor Lawn, but there was no sign of the oak tree.

Simon looked at his watch.

"The bus is due in five minutes. We'd better hurry," he said.

"Do we have to go back the way we came?" asked Steve.

"No. I know a short cut," said Simon, and he brought Steve down a lane which led back to the main road. They were halfway down the lane when they heard a familiar droning noise. It was the bus.

"It's early," said Simon, looking at his watch.

The boys ran down the lane as fast as they could. They could see the bus coming along the main road. It was getting nearer and nearer to the bus stop.

Suddenly, Steve stopped running.

"Simon," he shouted, "look at this!"

Simon glanced back at his friend. Steve was standing at one of the entrances to the housing estate, pointing at a road sign.

"What is it?" shouted Simon.

"Come here and look, quickly," Steve shouted in return.

Simon glanced at the bus. Too late, it was already pulling away from the stop. He walked back angrily to see what Steve was so excited about.

"Look," said Steve, pointing to the road sign.

"Big Oak Drive," read Simon. "So what?"

"Don't you see?" said Steve.

"See what?" asked Simon.

"This is the place," continued Steve. "This is where the oak tree must be."

"Don't be silly," said Simon, "it's only the name of the road."

"All the others are called Manor Estate something or other. This one isn't. It has to be the place," insisted Steve.

Simon thought for a moment.

"You may be right," he said.

"Let's go and look," said Steve.

"OK," agreed Simon. "We've missed the bus anyway."

6

The Map

"I told you it was just a name," complained Simon.

The boys had walked up and down Big Oak Drive twice, without seeing a sign of the oak tree.

"It has to be here," said Steve.

"Well it's not," insisted Simon. "We've searched high and low. There is no oak tree. In fact, there is no tree at all, except that ivy-covered thing beside the wall at the end of the road."

Suddenly Steve became very excited.

"That's it!" he exclaimed. "Why didn't I think of it before?"

"What's it?" asked Simon, but Steve was already gone. He was running at full speed down the road towards the ivy-covered tree.

Simon was out of breath before he finally caught up with Steve.

"What are you so excited about?" he panted.

"This is it," said Steve. "This is the tree. Look at the plaque."

On a wall beside the tree there was a small square plaque.

Simon began to read:

"This oak tree was planted in 1870 by the Earl of Monksfield to commemorate the building of the new wing to the Manor.

"When fully grown it had reached a height of 85 feet.

"On 28th November 1948 it was struck by lightning during a violent storm and had to be cut down for safety reasons."

"You're right," said Simon. "This is the tree, but there's not much of it left."

"It's still ten or twelve feet high," calculated Steve. "Look around for something to help us find the hole."

"Will this do?" asked Simon, holding up a stick about two feet long.

Steve took the stick from Simon and began to poke the tree firmly. The thick ivy covering made it difficult to find the hole. Once or twice the stick seemed to sink into the tree, but it was only soft bark. It was a slow process. Steve poked the tree, then moved a few inches and poked the tree again.

"Will this take long?" asked Simon, looking at his watch. "The next bus will be here in ten minutes."

"I don't know," said Steve. "I hope it won't take much longer . . ."

He had just spoken the words, when

suddenly the stick disappeared into the tree.

Steve tried to control his excitement.

"I think I've found it," he whispered.

"Let me see," said Simon.

Steve pulled away the ivy to reveal a small hole, just big enough for a hand to fit in. Slowly, he pushed his hand into the hole.

"Did you find anything?" asked Simon.

"Not yet," said Steve.

"Up and to the left," Simon reminded Steve of the instructions.

"I'm not tall enough," said Steve. "I need something to stand on."

Simon carried over the biggest stone he could find.

"Will this help?" he asked.

Steve stood on the stone.

"That's better," he said, and slid his arm deep into the tree.

"Did you find anything yet?" asked Simon again.

"I don't know," said Steve.

Slowly he pulled his closed fist out of the tree and let go the contents. Brown leaves, moss and rotten bark dropped to the ground.

Steve pushed his hand into the hole again and pulled out another handful. More brown leaves dropped to the ground.

"We'll have to go soon," said Simon, glancing at his watch, "or we'll miss the next bus."

"I'll just have one more go," said Steve.

Simon kicked the pile of dead leaves. Something square and shiny flew up in the air. Simon watched it flutter to the ground. It was a small plastic envelope. He picked up the envelope and opened it. Inside a piece of paper was carefully folded. Simon unfolded it just as carefully.

"Look, Steve," he shouted in excitement, "it's the map. We've found the map!"

"Sssh," whispered Steve, "keep your voice down."

Steve stared in disbelief at the sheet of paper in Simon's hand. It was true. It was the map.

"What are you doing there?" shouted a voice which made the boys jump.

It was a man across the road in his front garden.

"We're eh, eh, d . . . d . . . doing nothing," stuttered Steve.

"Get away from that tree," shouted the man again.

Simon quickly folded the map back into its envelope and put it in his pocket.

"I think we'd better get out of here," he said.

"And quickly," added Steve.

"Go on, clear off!" the man shouted after them, as the boys ran down the road.

"Keep going," panted Simon, when they reached the end of the road. "The bus will be along in a minute."

Gasping for breath, the boys reached the bus

stop just as the bus arrived. They slumped into the first vacant seat they found and slowly got their breath back.

"What will we do with the map?" asked Simon, when they got off the bus.

"I'll hide it in the wardrobe with the diary," Steve decided.

"Shouldn't we bring it to the police?" suggested Simon.

"We'll bring it tomorrow," said Steve. "I want to look at it before we hand it over."

"OK," agreed Simon, "see you in the morning."

Steve ran the rest of the way home. He knew his mother would be wondering what had happened to him.

"What kept you?" she asked, when he finally reached the house. "Your father's home from work already."

"I was with Simon," said Steve. There was no point in telling her about the map, he decided.

"You must be good friends," his mother said.

"We are," agreed Steve.

That night, before he went to sleep, Steve decided to have a good look at the map. He opened the plastic envelope and spread out the map on his bed.

The map meant nothing to him. In fact it was more like a set of instructions than a map. It was written in heavy pencil on a large sheet of discoloured white paper.

In the top left hand corner there was a drawing that looked like a castle. The words "East Tower" were written above it. A straight line with an arrow pointed from "East Tower" to a drawing of a church spire. The instructions, "Take 400 paces from East Tower", were written beside the line.

At the bottom of the page there was another drawing. Beside it the word "Well" was written. An arrow, coming from the other line, pointed towards the well. The instruction "Take 240 paces towards well. Here you will find the entrance" was written beside the arrow.

In the right-hand corner of the page were more instructions: "When you enter, keep to the left passage. Take forty paces. Entrance is on left. Go down steps to chamber."

"I'd love to go looking for the jewels," said Steve to himself, "but I suppose I'd better hand the map over to the police."

He folded the map and put it back into its envelope.

"I'll hide the envelope in the secret compartment of the wardrobe for safe-keeping," he decided.

7

The Red-Faced Sergeant

The following day was Thursday. It was Sports Day for Steve's class. Steve was in such a hurry getting his gear together that he forgot to bring the map to school. He was sitting down at his desk when he remembered it.

"I was in a hurry this morning and I forgot the map," he explained to Simon.

"We'll go to the police station anyway," said Simon.

It was almost five pm when the boys walked up the steps of the police station and through the main door into the hall.

Steve felt nervous as he pushed open the door of the Enquiries Office. A big red-faced sergeant with sandy-coloured hair was on duty behind the high counter. A tall man with dark curly hair was standing at the end of the counter looking at a map.

The sergeant leaned over the counter and looked down at the boys.

"Now what can I do for you?" he asked in a loud voice.

"We have a clue that might help solve a crime," said Steve.

"Oh! What kind of a clue?" asked the sergeant.

"It's a map," said Simon.

"Well, it's more like a set of instructions," added Steve.

"A map or a set of instructions," repeated the sergeant. "Tell me, where did you get this map or set of instructions?"

"We found it in an old tree," Steve told him.

The sergeant folded his arms and rocked back and forth. "You found a map or a set of instructions in an old tree." Again he repeated the boys' words.

Steve could see that he didn't believe them.

"Where is the map now?" asked the sergeant.

"It's in my bedroom," answered Steve.

"Oh!" said the sergeant. "Now tell me boys, when did this crime take place?"

Simon jumped in with the answer.

"1914," he said.

The sergeant threw back his head and roared with laughter. He laughed so much that tears ran down his red face. Steve thought the sergeant was going to burst, but he finally regained his composure. When he leaned over the counter towards the boys he had a big smile on his face.

"I may look old to you boys," he said, "but I can assure you that I wasn't around in 1914."

Once more the sergeant's loud laugh echoed round the small office.

"Mr Johnstone, what do you think of our two little sleuths here?" The sergeant addressed the man at the end of the counter.

"I think we have two new detectives," said Mr Johnstone with a smile. "They'll be after your job next."

The sergeant's big smile seemed to cover his whole face, but when he spoke again he was more serious.

"Lads, I am here by myself for the rest of this week and I'm very busy," he said. "I have a bundle of reports to go through and almost three hundred dog licences to check.

"I couldn't help you even if I wanted to. We only keep records here for five years. Anything older than that is held in our Central Records Division and believe me, I would have to have a very good reason to ask them boys to check back to 1914."

The sergeant paused for a breath. "I think the best thing you could do," he continued, "is to ask your teacher. Maybe he could do it as part of a history class."

Steve tugged Simon by the sleeve.

"This is a waste of time," he whispered. "Let's go."

"1914," repeated the sergeant again and once more he started to laugh. He was still laughing as the boys closed the door of the Enquiries Office behind them.

When they reached the main door, they

noticed that there was a big black cloud in the sky above them.

"I think we should run for it," suggested Simon, but just then a voice called them.

"Hold on a minute," shouted the voice.

It was Mr Johnstone.

"If you like, I could take a look at the map for you," he said. "I might be able to tell you if it is any good or not."

The boys looked at each other. Steve made the decision.

"No thank you," he said. "I'll hold on to it for a while."

"If you change your mind just give me a call," said Mr Johnstone. "I'm living at number twelve Moor Road."

"OK," agreed Steve.

"It looks like it could rain," observed Mr Johnstone. "Can I offer you a lift home?"

"No thank you," said Simon. "I only live down the road and Steve has just moved into Riverside Cottage on Cedar Avenue. It's not far."

"All right," said Mr Johnstone, "but if you get wet, it's your own fault."

Mr Johnstone went back into the Enquiries Office, leaving the boys to themselves.

As they walked down the steps, a man quickly moved away from the police station and disappeared around the corner. Steve recognised the man immediately. He had seen him across the road from his house the night before last. It was Walker.

8

Another Library Visit

"Who is Walker?" asked Simon.

"He moved into Mrs Gray's guest-house at the end of our road recently," said Steve, "but I don't know anything more about him."

"What do you think he wants?" wondered Simon.

"I don't know," said Steve, "but I'll bet he's up to no good."

Simon looked at his watch. "My dinner won't be ready for another hour," he said. "What'll we do until then?"

Steve glanced at the sky. "That cloud has moved away," he said. "We could go to the library and see if Mrs Faulkner has those old newspapers for us."

Mrs Faulkner was delighted to see the boys again, and just as Steve had hoped, she had the newspapers ready for them.

"Could I also have a look at the register of *Births, Marriages and Deaths*?" asked Steve.

"Of course," said Mrs Faulkner.

"What do you want that for?" asked Simon

when Mrs Faulkner had gone into the storeroom.

"I want to know what happened to the robbers," Steve told him.

"Why?" asked Simon.

"To know why they didn't come back for the map," said Steve.

Mrs Faulkner returned with a pile of old newspapers and the register, and put them down on the table.

"It's great to see you have such an interest in local history," she said to the boys. "You know, there are boys and girls in this town that never even come into the library, never mind reading up on local history."

Mrs Faulkner left the boys at the table and returned to the main desk.

"I have a lot to do this evening," she said, "so I'll leave you to it."

"Which should we start on?" asked Simon. "The register or the newspapers?"

"I'll start on the register," said Steve, "you start on the newspapers."

The boys sat in silence and slowly worked their way through the newspapers and the register.

Finally Simon smiled in triumph.

"Found it!" he said. "Look at this." He pushed the newspaper across the table to Steve.

The paper was dated 16th July 1914. The headline read: "Manor Robbery: Police Baffled".

Steve glanced through the article. There was nothing in it that they didn't already know.

"Take a look at this," said Simon, handing Steve another newspaper.

This one was dated 18th July 1914. There was a picture of James Clarke at the top of the page. Beside the picture the headline read: "Boy Disappears".

At the bottom of the page there was a picture of a man with curly hair and a beard. The name Jack Stone was written below the picture, and beside it there was a short article.

"The police wish to interview Jack Stone in connection with the recent robbery at Monksfield Manor and also in connection with the disappearance of local boy James Clarke," read Steve. "Stone is six feet two inches tall, weighs sixteen stone and has dark curly hair and a beard. He is believed to be dangerous. If you know where Stone is, you should contact the police immediately."

"Does that picture remind you of anybody?" asked Steve.

Simon looked carefully at the picture of Stone.

"No. He doesn't remind me of anybody," he said.

"I'm sure I've seen that face before," said Steve.

"Maybe it's somebody you knew in the city," suggested Simon.

"No, it's somebody here in Monksfield," said Steve, "but I can't think who it is."

"Did you find anything in the register?" asked Simon.

"Yes," replied Steve. "Something very interesting."

"What is it?" Simon asked eagerly.

"Barry, King and Rogers, all joined the army, and all were killed in action. King was killed on April 25th 1915 at Ypres. Barry was killed in the same battle two days later, and Rogers was killed on 3rd March 1916, at the Battle of Verdun."

"What about Stone?" asked Simon.

"That's the strange thing," said Steve. "There's no record of Stone. It's as if he just disappeared."

"He can't have disappeared," said Simon.

"I know," agreed Steve, "but wherever he went, he left no trail."

Simon looked at his watch.

"There's nothing more we can do here," he said. "Let's go home."

They closed the newspapers and register and stacked them in a neat pile at the end of the table.

"Did you find what you were looking for?" asked Mrs Faulkner.

"Nearly," replied Steve. "Do you know where we would get old maps of the area?"

"The Town Council have old maps," said Mrs

Faulkner, "but they won't let you borrow them. I used some of their maps in my book. You can borrow that if you wish."

"That would be great," said Steve.

Mrs Faulkner took her book *The History of Monksfield* from under the counter and handed it to Steve.

"Bring it back when you're finished," she said.

"Thanks very much," said Steve.

"What do you want the maps for?" asked Simon on the way home.

"We have the directions to the hiding-place," said Steve, "the police aren't interested . . ."

"So we'll look for it ourselves," interrupted Simon.

"Exactly," said Steve. "I'll look at the map tonight, and tomorrow we'll search for the entrance to the hiding-place."

9

The Break-In

Steve and Simon parted company at the end of Simon's road. As Steve neared his home, he noticed a group of people standing on the footpath. When he got closer he could see that they were standing outside his front gate.

I wonder what's going on? he asked himself.

"There was a break-in at your house," a voice behind him announced.

Steve turned around to see who had spoken. It was Mr Johnstone.

"He must have been looking for something in your bedroom," continued Mr Johnstone. "I'll help you check that everything is still there if you like."

Steve was too shocked to think straight.

"Eh . . . eh . . . eh . . . no thank you," he mumbled.

His mother was standing at the gate crying. She was being comforted by some neighbours.

Before Steve had a chance to talk to her, a police car pulled up and the big red-faced sergeant climbed out.

"What happened?" he asked, as he took a pencil and notebook from his pocket.

"When I opened the front door I heard a noise in the kitchen," sobbed Steve's mother. "I thought it was a dog or a cat, but when I went into the kitchen I saw a man climbing over the back wall."

"Did you get a good look at the man?" asked the sergeant.

"Yes," said Steve's mother. "It was the man who's staying in Mrs Gray's guest house."

"His name is Walker," volunteered a neighbour.

"Did anybody else see this man?" asked the sergeant.

"I saw him," said Mr Johnstone. "When I was coming up the road I saw him running away."

"Is there anything missing?" the sergeant asked Steve's mother.

"I don't know," she said. "I didn't get a chance to look. When I saw him climbing over the wall I just screamed and ran out."

"Let's go inside and take a look," suggested the sergeant.

While Steve's mother and the sergeant checked downstairs, Steve ran up to his room.

He pushed the bedroom door open slowly. He expected to see the worst, and he did.

"Oh no!" he exclaimed, as he looked around the room. "Mr Johnstone was right. My room is a mess."

Toys and books were flung out in the middle of the floor. Drawers had been emptied, and his clothes thrown out of the wardrobe.

Steve stared and stared at the wardrobe, until something suddenly clicked in his head.

The wardrobe, he thought in dismay, the map, the diary.

Quickly he grabbed a chair and jumped up on it. He felt along the shelf until his fingers found the knob. Slowly, he pulled the door open and slid his hand into the secret compartment. The tin was there, but was there anything in it . . .

Steve's heart pounded as he lifted down the tin. With shaking hands he pulled off the lid. He was afraid to look, so he squinted into the tin through half-shut eyes. A long slow sigh of relief whistled through his lips, when he saw that the diary and the map were still together as he had left them.

The sound of voices floating up the stairs told him that his mother and the sergeant were on their way up. Quickly, he put the lid back on the tin and returned it to its hiding-place.

"Oh no!" cried his mother, when she saw the mess. "Why did he do this?"

The sergeant glanced quickly around the room, as if summing up the situation.

"Looking for money, most likely," he decided. "Good job you came home when you did. He only got to search this room."

More likely he was looking for the map,

thought Steve.

The sergeant gave Steve a long hard look.

"Don't I know you from somewhere?" he asked.

Steve was just about to remind the sergeant of his visit to the station, when the sergeant came to his own conclusion.

"Of course," he said. "You were playing in goal against Brookfield last Saturday."

Steve's mother was so shocked, she didn't even hear the sergeant's remark, and Steve didn't bother correcting him.

"Nothing more I can do here," concluded the sergeant as he closed his notebook. "We'll pick up this Walker fellow quickly enough."

While Steve's mother phoned his father to tell him to come home early, Steve started to clean up the room.

What a mess, he thought, but at least he didn't get the map or the diary.

10

Clues Fall into Place

When his father came home, he helped Steve return the room to order.

"It looks all right now," he said when they had put everything back in its place. "Let's go down for something to eat."

When they got down to the kitchen Steve's mother was sitting at the table sobbing.

"I haven't got anything ready for dinner," she apologised.

"That's all right, love," Steve's father comforted her, "I'll put on the kettle."

"And I'll set the table," offered Steve.

Steve's mother barely ate anything, she just stared into her cup of tea.

"Why did it have to happen to us?" she asked for the umpteenth time. "I thought this was a nice town."

"It is," said Steve's father. "We were just unlucky, that's all."

Steve thought about telling his parents about the map and the diary, but he decided against it. His mother was still shaken and he didn't want to upset her any more.

I'll wait and see if the map leads anywhere, he decided, then I'll tell them.

After dinner, Steve rang Simon and told him what had happened.

"Oh no!" exclaimed Simon. "How did Walker know you had the map?"

"He must have overheard us at the police station," suggested Steve. "He left my room in a right mess, but it could have been worse. At least the map and the diary are still safe."

That night, Steve decided to go to bed early. He settled himself comfortably in his bed to look through Mrs Faulkner's book. Beside him, he had the directions he and Simon had found in the oak tree, and an up-to-date map he had borrowed from his father.

The book had a number of maps and pictures dating back as far as 1800. It was very interesting, but Steve didn't have time to read through it. He just wanted to find a map.

On page eight there was a map of the town of Monksfield dated 1845.

"That's no good," decided Steve. "What I need is a map of the whole area."

He flicked through some more pages which contained pictures of important local people from long ago.

Finally, on pages 28 and 29 he found a map of the whole area. It was dated 1910.

Just what I need, thought Steve.

He placed the directions, the book and his father's map side by side, and glanced from one to the other.

"I'll start by looking for the church spire," Steve decided.

It was easy to find the spire. There was only one church in Monksfield, and soon Steve had located it on both maps.

Finding "Tower" was more difficult. Steve searched both maps carefully, but he could find no tower or castle. The nearest thing he could find was an Abbey in an area called "Abbeylands" on the 1910 map. On his father's map it was marked simply as "Ruins", on a road called Old Abbey Lane.

Steve remembered seeing a drawing of the Abbey earlier in the book. He flicked back through the pages until he came to page seven. There he found a drawing of Monksfield Abbey dated 1870.

The front of the Abbey was built in the shape of a triangle, but at the back there were two square towers, one on each corner.

"That must be it," decided Steve.

Now began the search for the well. Again Steve searched both maps carefully, but this time he was out of luck. There was no sign of a well on either map.

He was just about to give up looking, when something strange on the map in Mrs Faulkner's book caught his eye.

At the bottom of the map a river was marked in. The river seemed to start beside a small road.

That's silly, thought Steve. A river can't just spring up like that.

Steve closed the book and dropped it to the floor. He straightened his pillows and let his head sink deeply into them. He had just closed his eyes, when suddenly the answer came to him.

"It's the well," he decided. "The well is the source of the river."

Steve jumped up and opened his father's map. The river was marked on it also. At the source of the river, the word "Mill" was written. It must be the well, thought Steve. The mill must be built on the well. The name of the road convinced him that he was right. It was called Clearwell Lane.

He lay back on the pillows again. He was very happy with his evening's work. All the pieces of the puzzle were beginning to fit together. Now all he had and Simon had to do was find the entrance.

11

A Dead End

At school the next day, Steve told Simon of his discovery, but Simon wasn't convinced.

"How do you know they are the right locations?" he asked.

"They have to be," said Steve. "They are the only ones that fit the directions. After school, I'm going to look for the entrance."

Simon thought for a while before he agreed to help.

"We'll start with the Abbey on Old Abbey Lane," said Steve.

Old Abbey Lane led the boys away from the town and into the country. Steve was very excited about the prospect of finding the jewels, but when they reached the Abbey, he couldn't believe his eyes.

His father's map had described the Abbey as "Ruins", and Simon had told him that the Abbey was in ruins, but Steve didn't expect it to be as bad as it was.

"I told you it's only a heap of stones," said Simon. "How are we going to find the tower?"

Steve said nothing. He just looked at the ruins and thought about the directions. From what was left of the Abbey, it was impossible to know where the towers had been.

"In the drawing in Mrs Faulkner's book there were two towers at the back of the Abbey," he said. "The tower we are looking for has to be on the side facing the town. Otherwise the robbers would not have been able to see the spire to pace out the directions. So it must be either this near corner or that far one over there."

"How will we know which corner is the right one?" asked Simon.

"We'll pick the one with the best view of the spire," decided Steve.

Steve climbed as high as he could on the broken wall and looked towards Monksfield.

"Can you see the spire?" asked Simon.

"Just the top of it," replied Steve. "Come on, we'll try the other corner."

The other corner of the Abbey was also in ruins, but there was something different about it.

"Look," said Steve. "See the way the stones are built in a square. This must be the tower."

From where they were standing, the boys were able to look down on the town. They could see the spire clearly.

"This has to be the place," decided Steve.

"So what are we waiting for?" asked Simon. "Let's go."

The direct route from the tower to the spire led the boys across several fields. Simon went on ahead, to keep them in a straight line, while Steve counted the paces.

"One, two, three . . ."

At 145 paces they came to a gate.

"I'll allow an extra pace for the gate," decided Steve. They climbed over the gate, and Steve continued his count.

"147, 148, 149 . . ."

They continued on a few paces.

"What are we going to do now?" asked Simon.

"219, 220," Steve stopped counting and looked up.

In front of them was a wide ditch of thorny bushes. There was no way through. Steve glanced around the field and then pointed to a gate in the corner.

"You cross over that gate and then come down along the other side of the ditch," he said. "I'll wait here until you are in position.

When Simon was in position, Steve went up to the corner of the field, crossed the gate and came down to meet him.

"I'll add in six paces for the width of the ditch," he said.

"That would be about right," agreed Simon, and he went on ahead again.

Steve continued to count out the paces.

"227, 228 . . ."

400 paces brought the boys to a small hollow in the middle of a big field. They could still see the Abbey, but they couldn't see the spire or the mill.

"This doesn't look right," said Steve.

"We counted out 400 paces," said Simon.

"I know," said Steve, "but it doesn't feel right. We can't see the mill, so how do we know what direction to go?"

Simon pointed to a small hill in front of them.

"I'll go up to the top of that hill," he said, "and stand between you and the mill. All you have to do is walk towards me."

"That's a good idea," agreed Steve.

When Simon reached the top of the hill, he waved to Steve to follow.

Once more, Steve began to count out the paces.

"One, two, three . . ."

He had counted to 115 when he reached Simon.

From the top of the hill the ground sloped away in front of them. They could see the mill clearly, but directly in front of them, there was a wood.

"We'll have to go through the wood to get to the mill," said Simon.

"You continue to lead and I'll count the paces," said Steve.

The trees were very close together, and progress through the wood was slow. After a while they heard a familiar droning sound.

"That sounds like traffic," said Simon.

Soon the trees began to thin out, and the noise of the traffic got louder.

All the time Steve counted out the paces.

"220, 221, 222 . . ."

Suddenly the boys stopped and stared in disbelief. Steve shook his head in dismay, but neither boy spoke. In front of them was the new motorway that bypassed Monksfield Town.

Simon was the first to speak.

"That's it then," he said regretfully. "The entrance and the jewels are buried under the motorway."

Steve searched for the right words to say, but none came to him. He was just about to scream with frustration and disappointment when a sudden noise in a bush behind them caused the boys to turn around.

Hurrying away through the trees was a man dressed in a dark jacket. The boys recognised him immediately. It was the same man they had seen running away from the police station.

"It's Walker!" said Steve.

"What's he doing here?" Simon wondered.

"He must have followed us," said Steve.

"Let's go home," said Simon. "Walker makes me nervous."

The walk home seemed very long, and the boys walked it in silence. They were too disappointed to talk, but something more than the disappointment was bothering Steve.

Walker must have known that we were searching for the jewels, that's why he followed us, Steve decided.

The thought of being followed around by Walker sent a shiver down his spine.

12

The Missing Link

"Would you like to come to the Video Library?" asked his father, when Steve got home.

"OK," said Steve.

Steve was still feeling disappointed, and he thought a film might help cheer him up.

When they got to the Video Library, Steve's father spent about ten minutes looking around before he finally picked a video.

"I have been waiting to see this for ages," he told Steve.

"What's it about?" asked Steve.

"It's Detective Lawson in his latest film," his father told him. "It's supposed to be very good."

Steve wasn't convinced. He didn't really like detective movies.

It was only a mile from Steve's house to the Video Library. Normally, it was a pleasant walk, but on the way home it started to rain.

"I think that we should walk a little faster or we'll get wet," his father suggested.

Although his father was still only walking, Steve found that he had to run to keep up.

"Do you always walk so fast?" asked a breathless Steve when they got home.

"It's just that I take longer steps than you," his father explained.

That evening they all sat down to watch the film.

Steve had to admit that his father was right. It was a very good film. He really admired Detective Lawson's persistence. Even when it looked like the clues had led him to a dead end, the detective didn't give up. He went over the clues again and again until he found the missing link and solved the case.

The film helped Steve to forget about his earlier disappointment, but later in bed the memories came flooding back.

The events of the day kept swimming round and round in his head. The directions, the ruins of the Abbey, counting out the paces, the motorway, walking back from the Video Library with his father, and Detective Lawson's persistence in looking for the missing link.

Even when he fell asleep, the same thoughts became a distrubing dream.

Normally on a Saturday morning Steve slept late, but this Saturday morning he woke up early. He was still thinking about the events of the day before.

Why do I keep thinking about walking back from the Video Library with Dad? he wondered.

Suddenly everything fell into place.

"Of course," he said to himself. "It's the missing link. Dad's steps were longer than mine. That's why I had to run to keep up."

Steve jumped out of bed and got dressed as quickly as he could. He was in such a hurry, he didn't even stop to wash himself.

His mother was reading the newspaper in the kitchen when Steve charged in.

"Where's Dad?" he asked.

"He's in the garden shed . . ."

Steve was already out the back door before his mother had finished speaking.

When Steve reached the shed, his father was opening a can of paint.

"What height are you, Dad?" panted Steve.

His father stretched himself to his full height and pushed out his chest.

"I'm six feet one inch tall," he said proudly.

Perfect, thought Steve.

"Will you do something for me?" he asked.

"I want to get the windows painted," said his father.

"Please Dad. It'll only take a minute."

"All right," agreed his father reluctantly. "What do you want me to do?"

"I'm conducting an experiment," explained Steve. "All I want you to do is walk from the shed to the back door and count the number of paces."

"One, two three . . ." counted his father, as he started walking. "Sixteen," he shouted to Steve, when he'd reached the back door.

Steve started from the same place.

"One, two, three . . . twenty," and he was standing beside his father. "Thanks, Dad," said Steve, and he ran back into the house, leaving a bewildered-looking father standing outside the back door.

"Do you want some breakfast?" asked his mother as he flashed through the kitchen.

Steve didn't stop to answer. He had already picked up the phone, dialled the number and was waiting impatiently for a reply.

"Simon," he said, when at last the phone was answered on the other end. "I know where we went wrong. Meet me in an hour up at the Abbey, and be prepared for a long search."

Before Simon had a chance to ask any questions, Steve hung up and went back into the kitchen.

"What's for breakfast, Mum?" he asked. "Oh, and I might be late for lunch," he added before his mother had had a chance to answer.

13

The Secret Entrance

Steve took a roundabout way to the Abbey, just to make sure that Walker wasn't following him. By the time he reached the Abbey, Simon was already there waiting for him. Steve had brought a spade, a rope and a torch with him.

"What's all the fuss about?" asked Simon, when he saw him coming.

"We measured the paces wrong," Steve told him.

"But we followed the instructions," insisted Simon.

"Stone was over six feet tall. His paces were longer than ours," said Steve. "I carried out an experiment with Dad this morning. For every four paces he took I had to take five."

"So for every four paces in the directions we should take five," concluded Simon.

"Exactly," agreed Steve.

Just then, a stone fell from the Abbey wall.

"What's that?" whispered Simon.

Steve went back to investigate, but he couldn't see anything. "It must have been a rabbit," he decided. "Come on, let's go."

Once more the boys began to count the paces. It was the same route as before, but this time they took 500 paces instead of 400.

Now, instead of being in a hollow, they were standing on top of a small hill. They could see the Abbey, the spire and the mill clearly, and the direct route to the mill would now take them around the wood rather than through it.

"Look," said Simon, pointing down the hill. "Who's that?"

A man moved behind a bush, as if trying to keep out of sight.

"He's probably a farmer," said Steve, but deep down he didn't believe that he was. Although he had been extra careful from the time he had left home, he still had the feeling that he was being followed.

"Is there something wrong?" asked Simon when he saw the worried look on Steve's face.

"No," said Steve, deciding not to tell Simon. There was no point in worrying him. "Let's go. We have another 300 paces to measure."

The boys walked down the hill and past the wood until they reached the Monksfield bypass.

"How are we going to get across?" asked Simon, as they watched the cars speeding up and down the motorway.

Steve looked both ways, then pointed in the direction of Monksfield. "There's a footbridge down there," he said. "We can use that to cross."

"How will we keep on line?" wondered Simon.

"Do you see that tree over there?" asked Steve.

"The one with the purply leaves?"

"That's the one," confirmed Steve. "Keep your eye on it, we'll continue our search from there."

The boys walked along the grass verge, by the side of the motorway, until they reached the footbridge.

"I'll keep a count of the paces," said Steve as they crossed the bridge.

"250," he said, when they reached the tree with the purple leaves.

The noise of the traffic died down as they moved further and further away from the road.

"This is it," said Steve, when he had counted out the last of the 300 paces. "The entrance has to be around here somewhere."

The boys were standing in a clearing between a small group of trees, and close to a high stone wall.

"Do you know where we are?" Steve asked Simon.

"I think this is the old cemetery," said Simon, pointing to the high wall. "It's just an old graveyard and a ruin of a church. Monks were buried here hundreds of years ago."

Suddenly, Simon dropped his voice. "It's supposed to be haunted," he whispered.

Steve felt a shiver run down his back, but it wasn't from the thought of the old church being haunted. He still had the feeling that they were being followed and watched. He glanced around nervously, but he couldn't see anybody.

"Let's start searching for the entrance," he decided.

"Where will we start?" asked Simon.

"I don't really know," said Steve. "The entrance could be anywhere. It might be best to start searching the ground first."

He pointed to one of the trees. "If you start over at that tree and walk up and down, and I start over here and walk across and back, we should cover the whole area," he explained.

The boys worked slowly and in silence. Steve used the spade to prod the ground, while Simon used a small branch he had found beside one of the trees.

"Help!" The silence was shattered by Simon's scream.

Steve spun around to find that Simon had almost disappeared down a hole. He was desperately clinging to a clump of grass that was already beginning to give way.

"Help!" shouted Simon again.

Steve rushed over to his friend and grabbed him by the arm.

"Get me out," pleaded Simon.

Steve pulled as hard as he could, but it was no use. Simon was too heavy for him to lift.

"I'm slipping," Simon cried.

The sound of stones and clay falling to the bottom of a deep hole echoed up to the boys.

Steve's arms ached. He couldn't hold on to Simon much longer. Suddenly, he remembered something his father had said to him when he was learning to swim.

"Kick with your feet," shouted Steve.

Simon kicked wildly. His toes slammed against something hard. A sharp and sudden pain shot through his foot and up to his ankle. Simon ignored the pain, and pressed his foot firmly against the hard object, then swung his other foot on to it and pushed up. His head came clear of the hole.

He reached a foot up higher and found another step. Again, he pushed with his feet, and his chest and shoulders came clear of the hole.

Steve grabbed Simon under the arms and heaved. Simon scrambled out of the hole and both boys collapsed on the grass in exhaustion.

"Phew! That was close," said Steve, after a while.

"What is it?" asked Simon.

Steve got to his feet. "It might be what we're looking for," he said, kneeling beside the hole.

"Look." Steve pointed to a piece of broken wood. "This must have been a cover over a hole," he said, "but it's all rotted away. That's why you fell through."

Simon viewed the hole from a safe distance and nodded in agreement.

"Hand me the torch," said Steve.

Steve flicked the switch and the bright torch beam flashed down the hole.

"This must be it," he almost shouted out the words in excitement. "There's a ladder with rungs all the way down to the bottom. This is the entrance. Now all we have to do is climb down."

"You go first," added Simon quickly. "I've been halfway down already."

Steve shoved the remains of the lid to one side, and started to climb down the ladder. He kept both his hands on the rungs and held the torch firmly between his teeth.

"Be careful," warned Simon, as the top of Steve's head disappeared down the hole.

14

Treasure Chest

"What's down there?" asked Simon, when Steve climbed back up again a few minutes later.

"There's an entrance to a long tunnel at the bottom of the ladder," panted Steve. "Drop down the spade and follow me."

A sharp "clang" resounded back up, as the spade hit against one of the rungs on its way down.

Steve had one more look around to make sure they weren't being followed. When he was satisfied that there was nobody around, he climbed back down the ladder again, closely followed by Simon.

"It's very dark," whispered Simon, as they watched the beam of the torch disappear into the blackness of the tunnel.

"Take forty paces and keep to the left, that's what the instructions said. So we have to take fifty paces," decided Steve.

"What do you think this place is?" asked Simon.

"Probably some kind of burial chamber for

the monks," said Steve. "A catacomb, I think it's called."

"Maybe we should go back," suggested Simon, in a voice that was starting to tremble.

Steve glanced at his friend. He could see that Simon was afraid, so he had to hide his own fear. He thought of a line he had heard in an old war movie and tried to sound as tough and as brave as he could.

"Come on," he said. "Let's move out."

Simon picked up the spade, and Steve counted the paces out loud. He found it helped control his fear.

"One, two, three . . ."

Simon sniffed loudly, and then his face screwed up as if he was in some terrible pain.

"What's that dreadful smell?" he asked.

"It's just dampness," said Steve. "Come on, let's keep going."

"Ten, eleven, twelve . . ." Steve continued to count out the paces, but now his counting was accompanied by a constant drip, drip, drip, as water seeped through the ceiling and dropped to the tunnel floor.

At twenty paces they came to a fork in the tunnel. Steve paused for a moment. The dripping sound was getting louder.

"Do you think the roof will fall in?" asked a worried Simon.

"It hasn't fallen in for hundreds of years, why should it fall in now?" Steve tried to sound reassuring, but he noticed that his voice had developed a nervous rattle.

Steve continued to count the paces out loud, as they made their way down the left-hand passage.

The dripping sound continued to get louder and louder, until suddenly the boys found themselves being showered with drops of ice-cold water.

Steve's breath caught in his chest from the sudden shock of the cold water. Beside him, he felt Simon hesitate.

"Not much further, we're nearly there," he managed to rasp out encouragingly.

At last the dripping stopped, and the boys stood cold and shivering in the tunnel.

"Hold on," said Simon, as he removed his glasses and wiped away the drops.

When he was finished, Steve continued with the counting.

"36, 37, 38 . . . 49, 50."

The boys stopped.

"The entrance should be here," said Steve, as he looked at the blank wall in front of him.

"Maybe it's a secret entrance," suggested Simon.

Steve pressed on the wall. His hand sank into something cold and slimy.

"What on earth!" shouted Steve, as he jumped back in fright.

"What is it?" asked Simon anxiously.

Steve moved the torch closer to the wall, until the beam shone directly on the spot where his hand had sunk into the green sticky slime that clung to the wall.

"It's only some kind of gooey fungus," he said, as he shook the slime from his hand. "Come on, let's keep looking for the entrance. I think I lost count when we were caught in that icy shower."

Six more paces brought the boys to a small opening in the wall.

"This must be it," said Steve excitedly.

"You go first," suggested Simon.

For a few moments Steve didn't move. A knot of fear turned in his stomach and he seemed to be stuck to the spot where he was standing. He wanted to turn back, but instead pushed himself into the narrow passage. We've come too far to turn back now, he thought to himself.

The light of the torch reflected off the walls and bounced back to dazzle him, and the walls themselves seemed to close in around him. In his stomach, the knot tightened and turned again.

"Stay close behind me," he said to Simon.

Luckily, the passage was short, and the boys soon found themselves descending narrow spiral steps.

Suddenly, the torch flickered, and then faded.

"What's wrong with the torch?" asked Simon nervously.

"I think the batteries are going," Steve tried to sound calm.

"Let's go back," pleaded Simon.

The torch flickered again. Steve felt himself starting to panic.

"Are you still there?" he called to Simon.

"I'm right behind you," came the reply, but Steve didn't find it reassuring.

Two more steps and Steve's feet landed on a smooth stone floor.

The fading beam of the torch flashed around a small empty chamber, until it landed on a pile of stones in the corner. Steve handed the torch to Simon.

"Hold on to this," he said.

With both hands, Steve pulled away the stones until he unearthed a small wooden chest.

"We've found it!" he shouted, and his excited laugh resounded round and round the chamber in an eerie echo. Steve pulled firmly on the lid of the chest, but it didn't move. He pulled again, but still it didn't move.

"It's locked," said Simon, as the torch beam picked out a small rusty padlock.

Steve picked up one of the stones and hit the lock firmly. There was a loud ringing noise, but the lock held firm.

"Hand me the spade," he said to Simon.

He slid the blade of the spade under the lid of the chest and leaned on the handle as hard as he could.

There was a loud creaking noise as the wood splintered, before the lid finally burst open.

The boys stared into the chest in disbelief.

It was full of jewels of every description, pearl necklaces, diamond rings and gold bracelets.

Steve was just about to pick up a handful, when a noise above him made him freeze. He looked at Simon. He too was staring up at the ceiling.

"Ghost!" whispered Simon.

The noise came again, and Steve knew that it wasn't a ghost. It was a footstep. This time it was followed by the groan of somebody squeezing through a narrow gap. More footsteps followed, and then a glow of light appeared at the entrance to the chamber. Somebody was coming down the steps.

A beam of a strong torch flashed first in Steve's, then in Simon's face, and finally landed on the open chest.

"So you found the jewels," said a deep gravelly voice.

Steve could only see a silhouette of the figure holding the torch, but he knew that figure well enough. It was Walker.

15

Underground Struggle

Walker began to move across the chamber towards the boys.

"Are you on your own?" he asked in his deep voice.

Steve's fingers closed tightly around the handle of the spade, as he swung it above his head.

"Don't come any closer," he warned.

Walker made a move to take something from his inside pocket, but he was interrupted by a sound above him. It was the sound of more footsteps. Somebody else was coming down the steps.

Quickly, Walker turned off his torch and pushed himself against the wall at the bottom of the steps.

"Don't say a word," he warned the boys.

A glow appeared in the entrance, followed by the sound of footsteps getting closer and closer. Once more the beam of a torch lit up the chamber and flashed from the boys to the jewels. It threw an eerie glow around the man who was holding it. Strange shadows flickered across his face, but Steve could still recognise the chubby features and curly hair.

"Well done, boys," came Mr Johnstone's familiar voice.

As his feet landed on the chamber floor, Walker made his move.

"Look out!" Simon shouted the warning.

Johnstone turned quickly, but not quickly enough.

"You . . ." was all he managed to say before Walker pounced.

Johnstone's torch fell from his hand, as the two men crashed to the ground.

Moans and groans came from both of them as they rolled around in a tangled mêlée. Fists and elbows flew in all directions.

There was a "clang" as a metal object fell and slid across the floor. Even in the fading beam of the boys' torch the shiny metal glinted. The boys stared at the object in horror. It was a gun!

"Ooh," groaned Johnstone, as Walker's fist crashed into the side of his head.

As Johnstone fell to one side, Walker struggled to his feet and staggered across the floor towards the gun. In a desperate attempt to stop him, Johnstone grabbed Walker by the ankle and sent him sprawling. Walker kicked his way free of Johnstone's grip and crawled towards the gun, but Johnstone flung himself across the chamber and landed on top of him.

Two hands stretched tantalisingly towards the gun. Walker's fingers closed around the handle and Johnstone's around the barrel.

The gun swung wildly as both men fought to gain control of it.

"Do something, Steve!" shouted Simon.

Steve tightened his grip on the handle of the spade and swung it as hard as he could.

There was a dull "thud", as the back of the spade came down on top of Johnstone's head.

For a few moments Johnstone seemed to freeze, then he rolled over and lay still.

Walker scrambled to his feet. There was a trickle of blood running down his forehead from a cut in his head. He rubbed the blood away from his eyes, then reached down and picked up the gun.

"Oh no!" cried Simon, "now look what you've done."

16

All is Explained

Walker rubbed more blood from his forehead with the back of his hand and put the gun in his pocket.

"How did you know?" he asked.

"I didn't," said Steve, "not until he walked down the steps. It was when the shadows fell on his face that I realised who he was."

"It was lucky for us that you did," said Walker. "He would have used the gun if he had to."

"What's going on?" asked Simon in bewilderment.

"I suppose I should introduce myself," said Walker, and he pulled a small identity card from the inside pocket of his jacket. "Detective Sergeant Tom Walker," he said. "Special Investigation."

"You mean you're the police!" said Simon in amazement.

"That's right," said Sergeant Walker. He reached into his trousers pocket and pulled out a set of handcuffs.

Johnstone was still unconscious, so it was easy to handcuff him. Sergeant Walker bent one of his legs up behind his back, pulled down an arm, and handcuffed his wrist to his ankle.

"That'll hold him until I get some help," he decided.

Sergeant Walker's powerful torch lit up the tunnel as the three of them made their way back towards the entrance. Somehow the tunnel didn't seem scary anymore, and soon they were out in the fresh air again.

Simon filled his lungs deeply.

"At last," he sighed.

"Is there a phone near here?" asked Sergeant Walker.

"As far as I know, there's a public phone at the end of Clearwell Lane," said Simon.

There was another field to cross before they got on to Clearwell Lane. Just as Simon had said, they found the phone at the end of the road and Sergeant Walker was able to call the local police.

"They'll be along in a few minutes," he said, when he finished the call. "You boys had better go home and tell your parents what has happened. I'll need you to come down to the station later to give a statement."

"OK," agreed the boys.

"How did you know about Johnstone?" asked Simon on the way home.

"When I saw him coming down the steps everything fell into place," said Steve. "I realised who he reminded me of. It was Stone. He looked just like the picture of Stone we saw in the newspaper, except without the beard."

"But wouldn't he be very old?" asked Simon. "I mean, the robbery took place in 1914."

"I don't mean that Johnstone *is* Stone," said Steve, "he's probably a relation or a descendant. I'm sure we'll find out exactly who is from Sergeant Walker later."

"So that old picture in the paper gave him away," concluded Simon.

"And his name, of course," continued Steve. "Johnstone, it's the same name as the original robber. If you break the name up, you get John Stone, and John is the same as Jack."

"That's right," agreed Simon. "Why didn't we think of it before?"

"We should have," said Steve, "or at least I should have, especially after the break-in at my house."

"What do you mean?" asked Simon.

"Johnstone knew that the robber had been looking for something in my bedroom," said Steve, "but he couldn't have known that unless he was the robber."

"That's right," said Simon, "but why did Walker act so strangely?"

"I suppose we'll find that out later on," said Steve.

"What do you think our parents will say?" wondered Simon, when they were almost home.

"We'll soon find out," said Steve.

Steve's mother was speechless when he told her what had happened. She was so relieved that nothing had happened to him that she forgot to give out.

"You shouldn't have gone searching for the jewels by yourselves," his father said.

"We didn't intend to," said Steve, "but we just got carried away."

His father nodded knowingly. "I understand," he said.

Later that evening, Steve and Simon and their parents met in the police station.

Sergeant Walker showed them into an interview room. The red-faced sergeant the boys had met at the station was also there.

"I suppose the boys have told you most of what has happened," said Sergeant Walker to the parents, "so I'll just fill in the gaps. My name is Detective Sergeant Tom Walker, and I'm attached to the Special Investigation Unit.

"We have had quite an adventure for the past week and, thanks to the boys, the Monksfield Manor jewels have been recovered."

The boys looked at each other and smiled with pride.

"It all started around the time of the First World War," continued Sergeant Walker. "A man named Jack Stone and his gang robbed jewels from the Manor. Stone escaped to Australia, but we don't know who the others were or what happened to them."

"They were killed in the War," said Steve.

"How do you know that?" asked his father in amazement.

"We looked it up," said Simon proudly.

Sergeant Walker laughed. "We have a right pair of detectives here," he said. "Anyway, Jack Stone never came back, so the case was closed, until about a month ago.

"The Australian police informed us that his grandson, Johnstone as he calls himself, was on his way over. The word was that he was coming to collect his inheritance, so we knew immediately that he was coming for the jewels.

"As soon as he arrived, I started to follow him, and he came directly here to Monksfield.

"Last Wednesday morning at about three am he went out. I thought he was going to get the jewels so I followed him, but he only went for a walk."

"That was when I saw you," said Steve.

"How did you see me?" asked a surprised Sergeant Walker.

"Something woke me up, and when I looked out the window you were across the street," said Steve. "A car came around the corner and I could see you in its lights."

"Johnstone almost saw me as well," said Sergeant Walker. "The next day, he came here to the police station to ask for directions to the Manor. While he was looking at a road map, you boys came in and told the sergeant here about the map you had found. The sergeant thought it was all a bit of a joke and didn't take you seriously.

The big red-faced sergeant blushed.

"Sorry, boys," he apologised.

"Johnstone, of course, knew all about the map," explained Sergeant Walker. "He knew that he had to have it in order to find the jewels. When you wouldn't give it to him, he decided to break into Steve's house and try to steal it, but he couldn't find it. How he knew where you lived I don't know."

"I told him," admitted Simon. "He offered us a lift home and I told him where we lived."

"It wasn't your fault," said Mrs Daly, "you didn't know who he was."

"Unfortunately, I was seen climbing over the back wall," continued Sergeant Walker. "My description was given to the police, so Johnstone thought he was off the hook.

"At that time, I thought that Johnstone knew where the jewels were, so I couldn't go to the local police in case they scared him off, but all his grandfather could remember was that the jewels were buried in a chamber somewhere between the Abbey and the old graveyard, and that the instructions to find them were hidden in a big oak tree on the Manor estate.

"Yesterday I followed Johnstone up to the Abbey and as far as the motorway. I couldn't understand why he was following you boys, but of course he was hoping that you would lead him to the jewels."

"We didn't allow for the fact that Stone was a lot taller than us and his steps were longer than ours," explained Steve. "So the map only led us to the middle of the motorway."

"This morning Johnstone followed you into the chamber, and I followed him, but somewhere along the line he must have got lost, because I ended up in front of him," said Sergeant Walker. "The rest you know."

"What will happen to the jewels?" asked Steve.

"They have already gone to the Museum," said Sergeant Walker, "but I'm sure you boys will get a reward. As for Johnstone, he will be spending the next few years in jail.

"Apparently this is the second time that his family have been denied the jewels by a boy. Johnstone's grandfather, Jack Stone, went back to collect the map the day after the robbery. He intended keeping all the jewels for himself and once he had the map, nobody else would ever be able to find them. But when he got to the tree there was a boy there before him. He pushed the boy away and the boy fell and hit his head."

"That must have been James Clarke," said Simon.

"James who?" asked Sergeant Walker.

"Just somebody who lived a long time ago," said Steve.

"Anyway," continued Sergeant Walker, "before Stone got a chance to get the map, a group of men arrived to work in a field nearby. Stone knew that they would see him if he went near the tree, so he crept away, hoping to come back later for the map.

"But by then the police were closing in on him and Stone wasn't able to get back for the map before he escaped to Australia."

The following day, the papers carried the full story, and a picture of the boys appeared on the front page. The boys were heroes, and when they went to school on Monday they were treated as such.

All the classes were called to the assembly hall to listen to the Headmaster praise the boys. Everybody cheered, even Maurice Brady congratulated them.

A week later, a cheque in the amount of £500.00 arrived for each boy from the Museum.

"Well Simon, do you still think that nothing ever happens in Monksfield?" asked Steve.

"Not likely," said Simon. "I wonder will anything that exciting ever happen to us again?"

"You never know," said Steve. "We could fall into another adventure at any time."

Also by Poolbeg

Shiver!

*Discover the identity of the disembodied voice singing
haunting tunes in the attic of a long abandoned house . . .*

*Read about Lady Margaret de Deauville who
was murdered in 1814 and discover the
curse of her magic ring . . .*

*Who is the ghoulish knight who clambers out of his tomb
unleashing disease and darkness upon the world?*

*Witness a family driven quietly insane by an evil
presence in their new house . . .*

*What became of the hideous voodoo doll
which disappeared after Niamh flung it from
her bedroom window?*

An atmospheric and suspense-filled collection of
ghostly tales by fifteen of Ireland's most popular
writers: Rose Doyle, Michael Scott, Jane Mitchell,
Michael Mullen, Morgan Llywelyn, Gretta Mulrooney,
Michael Carroll, Carolyn Swift, Mary Regan, Gordon
Snell, Mary Beckett, Eileen Dunlop, Maeve Friel,
Gaby Ross and Cormac MacRaois.

Each tale draws you into a web at times menacing,
at times refreshingly funny.

1 85371 300 7   £4.99